# For Flea, Sara, and James

First U.S. edition 1994
Published in Great Britain in 1994 by Walker Books Ltd., London.

Library of Congress Cataloging-in-Publication Data

Lewis, Kim.
The last train / Kim Lewis.—1st U.S. ed.
"First published in 1994 by Walker Books Ltd. ... London"—T.p. verso.
Summary: Sara and James imagine a puffing steam train rushing past their farm.
ISBN 1-56402-343-5
[1. Railroads—Trains—Fiction.   2. Imagination—Fiction.   3. Brothers and sisters—Fiction.]
I. Title.   PZ7.L58723Las   1994
[E]—dc20          93-32370

10 9 8 7 6 5 4 3 2 1

Printed in Singapore

The pictures in this book were done in colored pencil.

Candlewick Press
2067 Massachusetts Avenue
Cambridge, Massachusetts 02140

# THE LAST TRAIN

## KIM LEWIS

CANDLEWICK PRESS
CAMBRIDGE, MASSACHUSSETTS

On the old railroad line stood a hut. Railroad men used to have their coffee there when they worked on the line. But now the tracks were gone and the hut was empty.

That very hot summer, sheep used the hut. They rubbed their newly shorn fleeces against the walls and put their heads up the chimney to escape the flies. More and more gaps appeared in the walls. One day the door finally crashed to the ground.

Sara and James stopped on their bicycles to look.

"Let's make a camp," Sara said. She and James left their bicycles and clambered into the hut. They worked all morning, stuffing the cracks with wool and grass and stamping the dirt floor as flat as they could.

They leaned out the window and dreamed of the last train running through their farm. They thought they could see it, huge and puffing, as it rushed swift and mighty past the old hut. They thought they could hear it, horn wailing and wheels clattering fast on the tracks. They imagined being railroad workers and signaled to the driver as he sped by, high up in his cab.

But the wind blew through the gap where the door used
to be and the stuffing fell out of the cracks. The railroad hut
looked much as it had before.

"Some camp," declared James. They sadly wheeled
their bicycles home.

Mom and Dad were busy in the sheep pens.
They finished work to sit on the wall.

"The railroad hut is going to fall down soon,"
sighed Sara, slumping beside them.

"Will you help us save it?" pleaded James.

It was very hot, but they still set out, with tools
and scraps of wood, string and old carpet, bales of
hay, pots, and pans, all balanced on James's go-cart.

Sheep gathered to watch as the cart rumbled
along the railroad line to the hut.

Dad and James made a shutter for the window. Mom and Sara made a door. They used the hay bales for seats and laid scraps of wood and old carpet on the floor. They worked all afternoon, forgetting about time.

"Look!" James shouted to the waiting sheep. "Look at the Railroad Cottage now!"

Sara pinned her red handkerchief up by the fireplace.

"Whoever waves this when they stand by the Railroad Cottage will see a train," she said, "and the driver will stop."

Mom and Dad looked at each other and smiled.

"Tell us all about trains," said James. He and Sara snuggled up on the bales as evening drew in, very still and close.

Dad, who remembered steam trains, talked about when he'd watched them as a boy. Mom said she'd seen a photo in the village shop of a steam train stopped at the old village station.

The hot day darkened and a hush seemed to hold the air. Suddenly a gust of wind blew open the shutter.

James scrambled up and
leaned out the window.
Rain fell on his face.
A crack of lightning split the
hot air just as low rumbles
swelled from the hills.

Quickly Sara grabbed the
red handkerchief and flew
out of the Railroad Cottage.

James froze. In a thundering hiss of steam, a train with a wreath on the front blew out of the wind. He watched unbelieving as the train grew bigger and bigger, puffing slower and slower, steam billowing out over the railroad line. He saw Sara wave the red handkerchief. Rain hissed down on the hot train, spitting on the metal.

James raced out of the Railroad Cottage.
He and Sara took turns waving the red
handkerchief. They waved and waved.
The train brakes thundered and squealed.
The driver poked his head out the
brightly lit window, high up in his cab.
He smiled and waved back.

"Thunderstorm!" shouted Mom and Dad, stumbling out of the Railroad Cottage. Rain was falling in slanting, hard drops, faster and faster, pelting on the tin roof of the Railroad Cottage. Mom grabbed Sara and James's hands and pulled them along the railroad line, throwing sweaters over their heads.

In another flash of lightning,
Sara looked back. The Railroad
Cottage stood by itself, snug
against the rain, a last plume
of smoke curling out of
the chimney.

But the railroad line was
empty and the train was gone.

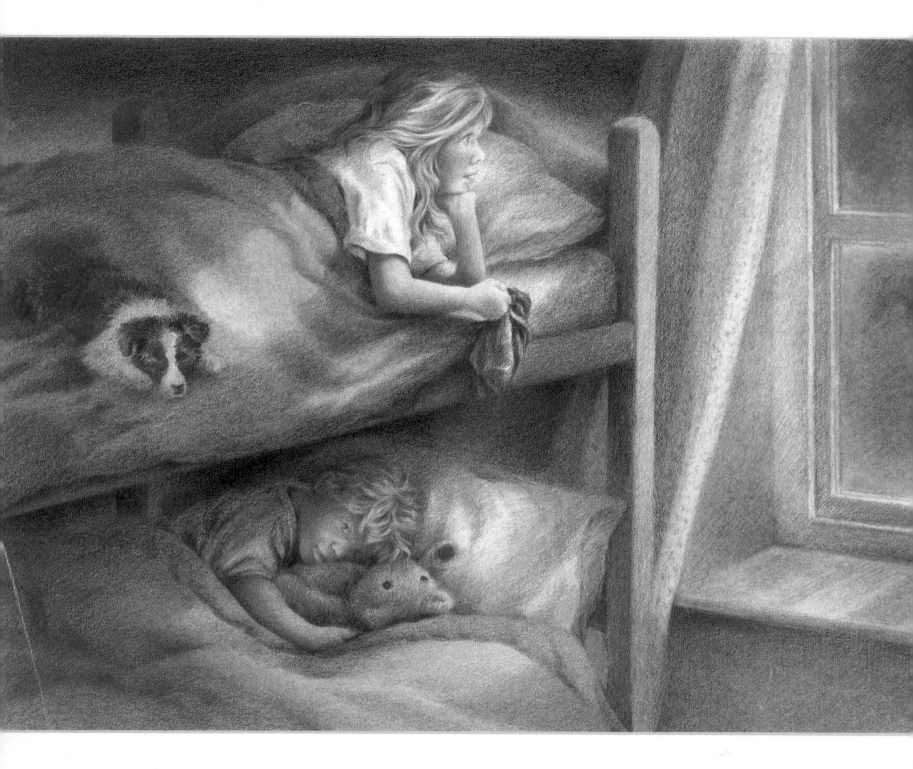

They shook the wet out of their clothes at home, shivering and laughing while it thundered and rained outside.

Mom and Dad tucked Sara and James into bed, but Sara could hardly sleep. She clutched the red handkerchief. James chattered excitedly, "We saw it! We saw the last train at the Railroad Cottage!"

Mom and Dad kissed them.

"Of course you did . . . " they said and smiled.

But Sara and James lay awake. They listened for trains in the rain and whispered to each other in the dark.